A Cow's
ALFALFA-BET

A Cow's
ALFALFA-BET

Woody Jackson

Houghton Mifflin Company Boston 2003

www.houghtonmifflinbooks.com

The illustrations are watercolor.

Library of Congress Cataloging-in-Publication Data
Jackson, Woody, 1948–
A cow's alfalfabet / by Woody Jackson.
p. cm.
Summary: Objects that make up life on a farm are depicted from A to Z.
ISBN 0-618-16599-1 (hardcover)
1. Farm life—Juvenile literature. 2. English language—
Alphabet—Juvenile literature. [1. Farm life. 2. Alphabet.]   I. Title.
S519.J235 2003   428.1—dc21   2002155545

Printed in Singapore
TWP 10 9 8 7 6 5 4 3 2 1

This book is dedicated to Eben,
who has brought gallons of laughter
and love into our world.

Alfalfa

Barn

Corn

Dog

Eggs

Flag

Garden

Hay

Icicles

Jerseys

Kittens

Lake

Moon

Night

ak

Pumpkins

Quack

Road

Snow

Tractor

Udder

Village

Woodpile

Xanadu

Yarn

Zucchini

A Cow's Alfalfabet reflects my love of the dairy farms in the Champlain Valley of Vermont and the people who farm them. It is an old-fashioned world of seasons and rhythms that are constant and comforting in a world of change and speed. Tractors move slowly, it takes patience to make hay, we are at the mercy of the weather. Yet to farm and herd celebrates our relationships with the land, our animals, and our families and neighbors. It brings us face to face with the earth and sky and the miracle of growing, not to mention the combustion engine. Since it has become a life that is financially difficult to sustain and not always convenient to our modern lifestyles, dairy farming is a disappearing existence. In each of these letters and pictures, I try to sing a few of its pleasures and hold it a while longer for our children.

—Woody Jackson